BOOK 2

THE KITTEN WHO CURED A GRUMP

NOVA DUBOIS

Printed in the United States of America
ISBN: 978-1-956019-53-7 (hardcover)
ISBN: 978-1-956019-54-4 (paperback)
ISBN: 978-1-956019-55-1 (ebook)

LCCN: 2022901385

Canoe Tree Press

4697 Main Street
Manchester Center, VT 05255
Canoe Tree Press is a division of DartFrog Books

Dedicated to all animals in shelters everywhere.
May they soon find their forever, loving homes.

4. Mr. Steve's house

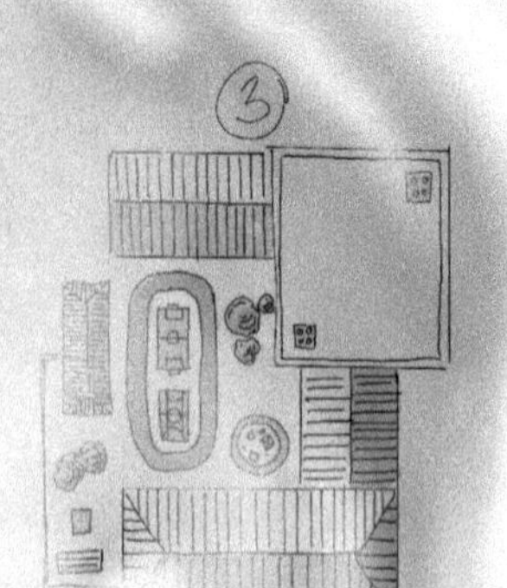

3. Makawee Elementary

2. Pebbles' house

1. Sweet Georgina's Chocolate Shoppe

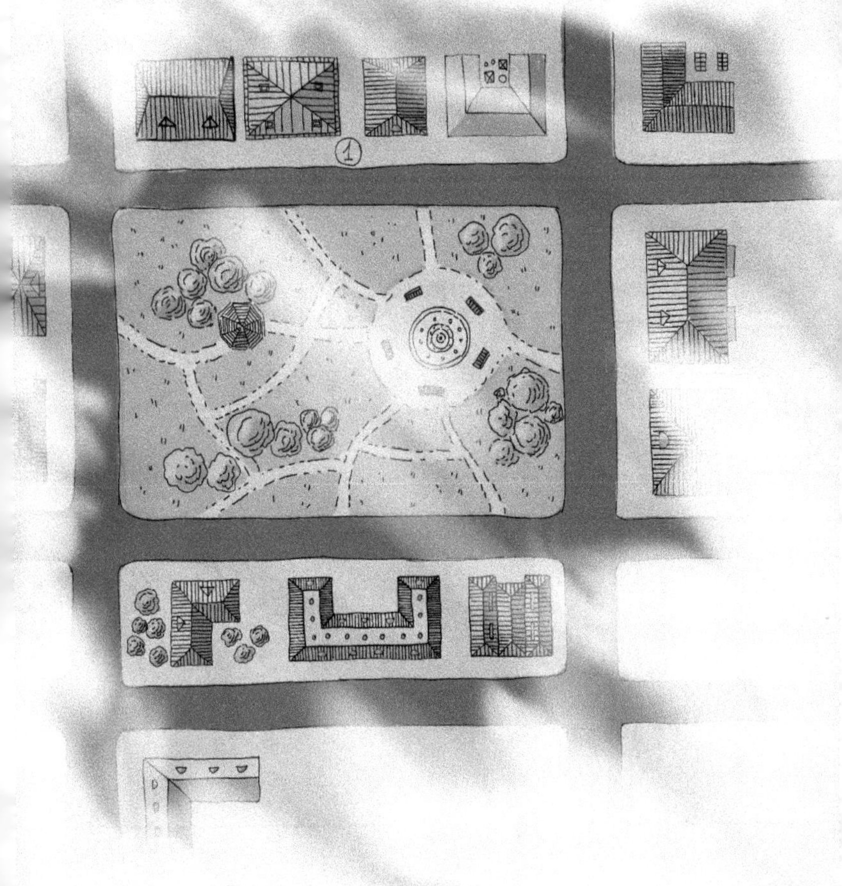

CHAPTER 1

GETTING READY FOR VALENTINE'S DAY!

I just love Valentine's Day! It's such a relief to have something to look forward to after the cold, dreary month of January. Every year, all the classrooms at school have a contest for the best-decorated Valentine's Day mailbox. Mom always supported Frankie and me with our projects by challenging us to think of creative designs and then helping us organize all the supplies we'd need. I'm proud to report we both have won the Best Mailbox Award.

Of all the Valentine's Day mailboxes we've created, my favorite is the one Frankie made last year. It was huge! Frankie made a green Transformer guy out of many cereal boxes. It had a wide-opened mouth where you could drop in your valentine. Dad is a dentist, and he let Frankie use some old plastic teeth to glue into the Transformer's mouth.

Frankie is my younger brother. My name is Ginni Pearl. I'm ten years old and in fourth grade, while Frankie is seven and is in first grade. We live with our father in a quaint little house in the town of Makawee.

Dad's dental practice is called Pearly White Dentistry. Frankie and I frequently walk to his office after school, and if he doesn't have a patient scheduled, he'll often go with us to the library. On rare occasions, we'll even get a Coke at the diner or walk the extra half block and get a fancy chocolate treat from Sweet Georgina's Chocolate Shoppe—but not too often, because it's Dad's job to help keep residents of Makawee free of cavities and root canals!

This year, Frankie and I are on our own with our Valentine's Day mailboxes. Mom died last summer. She didn't get sick or anything. She died when her plane was shot down. Mom was a fighter pilot until that fateful mission. I will always remember standing by her graveside next to Dad and Frankie with Dad holding the folded American flag that had covered her casket. Sometimes I wish she had been a teacher or a nurse or something, because then she probably would not have died. But I know Mom would be disappointed in me if she knew I thought that. A lot of relatives on Mom's side of the family were and are in the military, and she was extremely proud to serve her country. And although it hurts, I'm proud of her and her family's legacy, too.

It was Saturday afternoon, and Frankie and I were discussing what we were going to do this year for our Valentine's Day mailboxes. We were at the kitchen table, and we each had notepaper in front of us, sketching out ideas.

"How about something like this?" Frankie said as he showed me his drawing of a shoebox turned into a black cat. It had ears, a tail, and even whiskers.

No surprise there, I thought, smiling to myself as I looked over his drawing.

Neelia is our darling black kitten. She joined our family two months ago on Christmas Eve under the strangest circumstances. Her arrival had been announced by flickering lights, Alexa turning on by herself (playing Mom's favorite Christmas melody), and Tyto, a friendly barn owl, knocking on our door with his beak to call us outside. Frankie was the first to see Neelia, huddled in the snow under our maple tree. He rushed to her in his bare feet. With Frankie's pleading eyes, Dad allowed us to bring her indoors. And she has hardly left Frankie's side ever since.

"Frankie," I replied, "that's perfect! And here's what I'm going to create."

I showed him my drawing of a Valentine's Day box made into a mouse. My drawing showed a shoebox with mouse ears, a pink tail, and extra-long whiskers. Mr. Whiskers, my pet mouse, also joined our family over last Christmas break. He had been hiding somewhere in the house and kept stealing small objects. At first, we thought it might be Neelia, but Neelia solved the culprit mystery by trapping him under the Christmas tree skirt. Surprisingly, the kitten and the mouse have become great friends.

"Let's take a break, Frankie, and go to Sweet Georgina's Chocolate Shoppe to order Dad's favorite Mint Meltaways before she closes," I said. "Remember last year? She sold out, and Dad never got his Valentine's Day treat."

I shouted to Dad, who was working in his home office, that we were going on a quick errand downtown and we'd be back soon.

"If you stop by the Yummy Tummy Grocery Store, you could pick up some fresh French bread, and I'll make spaghetti and garlic toast for dinner tonight," Dad called back. "Take a couple of bucks from the teapot."

"You bet!" we both shouted back. Dad's spaghetti is the best! And his toast drips with melted garlic butter.

While I dug in the teapot for some cash, Frankie got down Neelia's harness and leash that hangs by the back door. As soon as she heard her leash rattle, Neelia sprang off her kitchen chair and rubbed against Frankie's legs while he fitted her with the harness.

Neelia is the only cat I know that loves to walk on a leash. She seems happy to do most anything as long as she can stay with Frankie.

Keeping money in a teapot was Mom's idea. That way Frankie and I could have easy access to some cash when we needed to pick up something for the house. There was a time when just lifting the lid off that teapot would send tears running down my cheeks, because it reminded me of her. In the weeks and months following her death, every time I turned a corner, there was something that reminded me of Mom. I clearly remember Mom's standing there laying down the rules of the teapot cash and putting me in charge. I was so proud. But now, I can think of Mom and have it fill my heart with love instead of grief.

I know time has helped to lessen the grief, but to be honest, I owe much of the healing to Neelia. All of us are in a better place since Neelia joined our family. She makes us laugh when she plays, she gives great kitty hugs and kisses, and when she naps on your lap, you can't help but feel comforted.

That Neelia's black fur is a perfect match to Mom's beautiful hair,

. . . and the collar she was wearing when she arrived was Mom's favorite color,

. . . and that she sits in Mom's chair at mealtime as if she belongs there,

are all unexplainable connections to Mom.

"Let's go," I said to Frankie as we zipped up our winter jackets and slipped on our boots. While many store-bought calendars have spring flowers displayed for the month of February, not so in Makawee. February is still the dead of winter, and we always have at least six more weeks of snow and ice after Groundhog Day, no matter if Punxsutawney Phil sees his shadow or not.

With Neelia leading the way (how she always knew where we were heading, I'll never know), we were off, with Tyto, flying right behind us. I heard a faint whirring noise, but when I looked around, there was nothing there.

"Good thing Neelia is taking us to the chocolate shop first," I commented. "The chocolate shop closes earlier than Yummy Tummy."

"Frankie, look," I cried as we got close to the store.

Frankie looked at me and then glanced in the direction of my stares.

"What's the Closed sign doing on the front window, Ginni?" asked Frankie. "It's not even three o'clock yet."

"I don't know," I replied. "Say, there's Dr. Little coming out of the cell phone store. Let's see if he knows."

We hurried our pace to catch Dr. Little before he got into his car, and as soon as he saw Neelia, he broke out into a huge grin.

Dr. Little is Mawakee's veterinarian. Over Christmas break, he was the one who gave us the great news that Neelia was not microchipped. But he also told us to think about what we'll do if a previous owner should claim her in the upcoming weeks or months. I'm praying we never will have to make that decision.

"There's my little sweetheart," he said as he tickled Neelia under her chin. While Neelia gets along well with almost everyone, she seems to really love Dr. Little. "How's our girl doing?" he asked.

"She's purrrrfect," Frankie said with a laugh.

Dr. Little laughed back.

"Dr. Little," I asked, "do you know why Sweet Georgina's Chocolate Shoppe is closed?"

Dr. Little looked over and noticed the Closed sign. "No, I don't," he said. "But it seems rather odd for her to be closed in the middle of a Saturday afternoon. Isn't she usually open until five o'clock?"

Frankie, with Neelia in tow, ran to the front door to check. "Yep," he shouted back. "The sign says 9:00 to 5:00 on Saturdays."

"I hope Georgina is feeling okay. I suspect she'll be open tomorrow. Going to get your boyfriend some chocolates, Ginni?" teased Dr. Little.

I blushed while Frankie came to my rescue. "We

were going to order Dad his favorite candy because last year she sold out."

"Well, okay, then," Dr. Little said back to me with a wink. "Guess you'll have to try her tomorrow."

As Frankie turned to start walking home, I called out, "Hey, Forgetful Head, what about the French bread?"

"Oops," Frankie laughed as he turned around to join me. What he didn't notice was when he turned to walk toward home, Neelia didn't follow him but instead sat down facing toward Yummy Tummy.

Just how does she do that, I wondered.

CHAPTER 2

WHO'S THERE?

As we were walking home from church services Sunday morning, I had a strange feeling, and it wasn't the first time. I had the sense that we were being followed. I first felt this on our trip to the chocolate shop, but today, the feeling was stronger. Just like the day before, I thought I heard a slight whirring noise, but I never saw anything when I looked around.

"What's going on, Ginni?" asked Dad. "You seem jumpy."

I didn't want Dad to think I was being silly, so I simply said, "Oh, I'm just eager to get out of my dress clothes and spend some time with Mr. Whiskers and get started sewing hearts on my Valentine's Day t-shirt."

Dad looked at me quizzically, but he said nothing more.

But then the whirring noise happened again. The hairs on the back of my neck stood up.

"Look, there goes Tyto!" shouted Frankie.

I looked up. Yep, it seemed Tyto had followed us home from church. Could the whirring noise have been Tyto's wings all along? He had just landed on his favorite perch in the maple tree—the same one he'd sat on when he showed us Neelia for the first time last Christmas Eve. I'm sure I was imagining things, but I could have sworn Tyto didn't look happy.

"Dad, would you mind if Frankie and I stop over at the Pebbles' while you finish making Sunday dinner?" I asked. Dad had put a roast in the oven before we left for church, and I knew it would take him some time to finish with the potatoes, gravy, and vegetables. "We haven't seen them all weekend."

"Sure," said Dad. "But I thought you were eager to get out of your Sunday best and spend some time with Mr. Whiskers and start sewing."

"Oh, this won't take us long—just a quick visit," I said.

"Okay, I'll turn on the football game to keep myself company. But don't be too long," said Dad.

"Great," I said, and I grabbed Frankie by the arm. "Let's go, Frankie. We can come back and change our clothes after we spend some time next door."

"Can we take Neelia?" Frankie asked.

I gave a slight sigh with a smile and said, "Of course we can. Neelia is always welcome at the Pebbles'."

My best friend, Catherine, lives with her two sisters (Sharnelle and Rose) and their mom next door in a home that looks like it could be sitting on a Caribbean island. As it should. The Pebbles family moved to Makawee from Jamaica, and I love everything they've shared with us about their Jamaican culture. Ms. Pebbles is the Director of Nursing at Makawee General Hospital, and it's often very handy to have a nurse next door.

But when Frankie got back outside with Neelia harnessed up, Neelia and I started heading for downtown instead of next door.

"Ginni, are you nuts?" asked Frankie. "Did you forget the way to Catherine's?"

"Shh," I said. "I don't want Dad to hear us. A visit to Catherine's was just an excuse to get out of the house. Let's go back to the chocolate shop now and see if it's open. I even thought of this before church, and I stuck our Valentine's gift money in my pocket."

"Pretty sneaky," Frankie complimented with a grin.

It's an easy walk to the chocolate shop, and we were there in no time. As we quickly found out, we weren't the only ones who made this trip on Sunday afternoon—I guess many people had been disappointed when Georgina's was closed yesterday.

"Wow," Frankie said. "I've never seen it so packed in here."

Not only was it packed, but Georgina wasn't acting like her normal self. "Speak up," she barked to a young girl at the counter. "I can hardly hear you." I saw the little girl's mother pick up her scared daughter and repeat to Georgina what they wanted.

Right after she rang up the sale, Georgina, with a scowl on her face, hollered, "Who's next?"

"Frankie," I whispered in his ear, "let's go home and come back tomorrow after school."

Frankie's eyes were wide. He, too, had never seen Georgina act this way before. He simply nodded, and we snuck out the door for home.

When we got about a block away, Frankie asked me what I thought was wrong with Georgina.

"I don't know," I said. "Maybe she's still not feeling well, and it has to be tough to wait on so many impatient people. But I have never seen her act that way. Usually, she's laughing and making everyone feel special when they're in her store. It probably won't be as busy after school tomorrow. I'll be eager to see how she is then. But we have to get Dad's chocolates ordered before it's too late!"

I took Frankie around the block south of Vine Street so we would approach the house as if we were coming back from the Pebbles'. "Pretty sneaky again!" said Frankie when he figured out why we were walking home that way.

Right before we got to our yard, I heard the whirring sound once more. And I had a feeling we were being followed or at least watched. I started twirling a few strands of my long red hair.

"Oh, boy! A mystery?" Frankie asked.

I had a habit of twirling my hair when I was in the middle of a mystery. But there wasn't a mystery here, was there? I laughed nervously. "No, I don't think so. Let's hurry inside, change our clothes, and help Dad get Sunday dinner on the table. I hope the roast is tender," I said to Frankie as we ran up the front steps.

"Please pass the chili sauce," I asked as I took my second helping of the roast.

"You're just like your mom," said Dad with a fond look on his face. "She loved that stuff on her beef and pork roasts, too."

"It's always a toss-up," I explained. "I love your gravy as well. That's why the first helping is with mashed potatoes and gravy and the second helping is with chili sauce."

Dad laughed. "I'm glad you have a system in place!" As we began cleaning up the table, he asked, "How are the girls?"

"Huh?" I asked.

"Catherine and her sisters . . ." Dad prompted.

"Oh, sorry," I quickly replied. "Everyone's A-OK over there."

Geesh! I was going to have to keep my wits about me. Being sneaky is hard to do; you have to be really careful not to make mistakes. Right after the dishes were in the dishwasher and the crumbs were swept away, I grabbed my phone and texted Catherine.

Hey, if Dad should ever say anything about Frankie and my stopping over after church today, please tell him we were there for just a little bit.

Ok...???

Nothing bad. Instead of going to your place, Frankie and I went to the chocolate shoppe to order Dad's favorite candy for Valentine's Day. She ran out last year and we want it to be a surprise.

Lol. Ok, cool. Happy to be part of a ♥ Day surprise. Got your classroom mailbox done yet?

Not yet, but we're going to work on them this afternoon.

I love having a cell phone. Over Christmas break, Frankie and I had gone sledding with the girls at Totem Trails Park, and Frankie had sprained his ankle. That's what finally convinced Dad that I should have my own cell phone. Fortunately, Neelia had known something was wrong at the park and convinced Dad to drive over and check it out. Good thing, too. It would have been a long walk carrying sleds and trying to help Frankie hobble home. I guess Dad decided he couldn't always count on Neelia for emergency notifications—although I wouldn't bet against Neelia.

It was about bedtime, and I was finishing appliquéing some hearts on a t-shirt I was going to wear to school on Valentine's Day, when I looked up and saw a strange light in the backyard. It was like a flashlight, but it was as if the flashlight beam was coming from above. As soon as I stood up and walked to the window, the light vanished.

Was I seeing things? Was I simply tired and my eyes strained from the appliqué work? I couldn't swear that I really saw what I thought I saw. I shook my head, went over to Mr. Whiskers, and picked him up.

"Am I going crazy?" I asked. To answer me, he simply crawled up my arm, snuggled in close to my neck, and tickled me with his long whiskers. I laughed and, surprisingly, felt better.

"Okay, little guy," I told him. "Time for both of us to go to sleep." But after I tucked him into his snug little cage, I glanced out the window one last time before I crawled into bed. All I saw was Tyto circling around the backyard.

"All clear," I said to myself as I turned off the battery-powered tea light candle on my nightstand. Mom and I used to light a candle when we sewed together and worked on crafts, and it comforted me to keep this tradition.

I tried not to think about the strange light and the feelings of being followed as I twirled my hair and fell asleep.

SCHOOL

CHAPTER 3

BACK AT SCHOOL

On Monday morning, Frankie and I carried our Valentine's Day mailboxes to school in paper bags. We had finished them on Sunday night. Even without Mom's help, I had to admit they turned out pretty cute.

Frankie had covered his box with black felt to make the box look like fur. Then I showed him how to cut out a strip of felt for the tail and four triangles for ears. I took the strip of felt and sewed it into a tube, and Frankie stuffed the tube with cotton and attached it to the felt-covered box. After that, I sewed the triangles together to make two ears, and Frankie stuffed them also with cotton and glued them on. Frankie was pleased with how it turned out.

Recently, Catherine called me "the woman of the house." Even though I didn't understand at the time what being the woman of the house means, when Frankie hugged me after I helped him with his Valentine's Day mailbox, Catherine's comment came to mind. Maybe part of being the woman of the house means helping everyone with what they need. Maybe.

My "Mr. Whiskers" mailbox turned out pretty well, too. I used gray construction paper to cover my shoebox. I found some gray pipe cleaners in one of our craft boxes, and I cut it to whisker length and glued it to Mr. Whiskers' face. That really made the box cute.

I didn't think either of us was going to win the Best Mailbox Award this year, but I knew both our mailboxes symbolized the love we had for our pets. And no one could love their pets more than we did. And after all, isn't love what Valentine's Day is all about?

We had just turned to walk up the sidewalk to school when we heard Rose and Catherine call out to us, "Hey!" and "We want to see your Valentine's Day mailboxes!"

Frankie left my side and ran over to Rose to walk into school with his friend. I saw him open the bag and show Rose his mailbox. She clapped her hands and laughed with glee. That's a good sign, I thought.

Catherine and I walked into school together. Of course, Catherine loved my Valentine's Day mailbox. But I thought this year Catherine had a chance to win the Best Mailbox Award for her classroom. She had gone into great detail and made her Valentine's Day mailbox into a vet clinic. Since second grade, Catherine has known she wants to be a vet. Her mailbox was made from a shoebox mounted on a piece of cardboard. The box had windows cut into it with itty bitty cats that sat on the windowsills. A sign next to the box read "Pets' Favorite Vet Clinic." On the cardboard, Catherine had made a sidewalk with a walkway leading to the clinic. She also had attached a toy fire hydrant near the sidewalk and had a miniature dog lifting its leg on the hydrant. Clever Catherine!

"This is getting heavy," Catherine said as she brought me out of my thoughts. "I'm going to hurry to my classroom. See you at recess."

Just as Catherine scooted into school, I heard a sneering voice say, "Hey, Red."

The voice was none other than Stanley's. While the Pebbles live on the west side of us, Stanley's family lives on the east side. Lately, I've noticed how often Stanley's left alone. I'm beginning to agree with Dad that Stanley must be pretty lonely. But Stanley seems to take his loneliness and turn it into being a bully. I did my best to not let him get under my skin.

"Good morning, Stanley," I said coolly.

"Got your Valentine's Day mailbox there, I see," Stanley scoffed. "Aren't you getting a bit too old for such things?"

"Well, I see you're carrying a mailbox for Valentine's Day," I said. "If you think we're too old, why'd you make one?"

"Well, some of you numskulls actually put candy in with your valentines. I'd be a fool not to rake in the loot," he said.

When I looked closer at Stanley's mailbox, I could see all he had done was sloppily cover a shoebox with black construction paper. Not a heart or decoration on it. *Black, like his heart*, I thought.

"Are you busy supporting our local candy store these days, Carrot Top?" Stanley continued. "Two trips in one weekend? Got a sweet tooth, have ya?"

Before I could tell him it was none of his business, he ran off to join one of his cronies.

Then something occurred to me. How did he know

I had been to the chocolate shop twice over the weekend? I hadn't seen him around during either of our trips. And neither had I seen him standing at his picture window, looking out like he often did when he was home alone. Stanley's a big kid. I couldn't imagine he could sneak around unseen and unheard. But was this what I had been feeling lately?

Almost everyone had brought their mailboxes today. We still had over a week to go before Valentine's Day, but since many kids brought their valentines in early, you didn't want to miss the early-bird valentines with possible treats inside.

It took Ms. Zinger, my teacher, longer than usual to settle us down. Everyone loved seeing the Valentine's Day creations. When Ms. Nineon, our school principal, came on the intercom with the Monday morning announcements, we all quickly scooted to our seats. Ms. Nineon is a pretty tough principal, and even over the intercom, you feel like she is watching you.

When our day was done, Catherine and I waited outside the school to meet the others. The first to arrive was Sharnelle. "Hey, Sharnelle," I asked, "what was your Valentine's Day mailbox this year?"

"Guess," she said.

"Did you make it into a white rat?" I asked. Sharnelle has a white rat for a pet. While I love Mr. Whiskers and enjoy snuggling with him, I couldn't get my head wrapped around the idea of a rat for a pet. It must be that long, fat tail.

"Nope," she answered. "I covered my box with

green paper and put a track on the top of the box and glued little track runners onto it. I cut a slot for the valentines in the middle of the track."

"Pretty cool," I told her. Sharnelle has always wanted to run for the high school track team. I often see her in the neighborhood as she races by in her running shoes.

Just then Frankie came out of school, followed by Rose, and the five of us walked home. We dropped the girls off at their house and went home to get ready for our third trip to the chocolate shop. My mind went back to the conversation with Stanley that morning. Would he be watching me on this trip, too?

EVICTION NOTICE

CHAPTER 4

EVICTED

Frankie and I laid our homework on the kitchen table to be completed while Dad made dinner. Then we ran upstairs and changed our clothes for the trip to the chocolate shop. Frankie harnessed Neelia, and we were on our way.

It felt like we were on autopilot—we had been going to the chocolate shop so often lately. Tyto was accompanying us like he usually did. As I expected, the chocolate shop wasn't busy this afternoon. In fact, no one, not even Georgina, was in the store when we entered.

"Hello," I cried out as both Frankie and I pressed our noses against the glass-covered candy displays. Georgina had so many types and styles of chocolates, it was almost impossible to have only one favorite.

"Frankie," I said, "I brought along some extra money from my allowance. You and I both can pick out one chocolate treat."

"Thanks!" said Frankie with a big grin.

We both searched the displays while Neelia started doing her own search. In just a few minutes, Georgina came out from the back office and briskly said, "Can I help you?"

"I'd like one Sea Salt Dark Chocolate Caramel, and I bet Frankie would like one Peppermint Buttercreme," I replied while looking over at Frankie.

Frankie nodded his head yes and smiled.

"Will that be all?" Georgina asked with a sigh.

"No," I said. "We'd also like to order your specially wrapped Valentine's Day box filled with Mint Meltaways for our father. When can we pick it up?"

"I'll have all orders ready for pickup on the thirteenth," Georgina said curtly. "Say, what's that cat doing in here?"

"It's just Neelia," Frankie whispered. "I'll take her outside if you don't want her in here."

"Yes, get that cat out of here!" snapped Georgina.

Frankie quickly went over to Neelia, who was coming out from behind the counter. He picked her up and carried her out.

I paid for all the chocolates, told Georgina I'd be back on the thirteenth to pick up Dad's order, and followed Frankie out the door.

Frankie and Neelia huddled while he sat on the curb. I couldn't tell if he was comforting Neelia or if Neelia was comforting him.

"Look," he said as he handed me a wadded-up piece of paper. "Neelia had this in her mouth when I picked her up. She must have found it somewhere behind the counter. I was too scared to go back inside and give it to Georgina. What is it?"

I didn't want to go back inside either, so I took the paper, straightened it out, and looked it over. It looked very formal and official, and I couldn't read all the words.

"I don't know," I said to Frankie. "Let's ask Dad when he gets home. Want your piece of chocolate?"

"Nah, I don't feel like it," answered Frankie. "Let's save our treats for dessert."

Frankie was such a tender-hearted kid, and it just killed me when someone yelled at him like Georgina had. *What is going on with her?* I wondered.

"Come on, let's head for home and get our homework done early. That way, we can talk about this with Dad before dinner and not have to have him nag us to get our homework done," I said.

Was that whirring I heard as we walked toward home? Again, I looked all around and saw nothing. I had too much on my mind to worry about something I couldn't see, so I made myself forget about it as we trekked home. But I saw Tyto flying behind us. While he often accompanies us when we're out, he'd been following us more than usual lately.

We had just closed our books when Dad shouted, "Hey kids, I'm home!"

"Hi, Dad," I called back to him. Frankie was still a little glum and didn't answer Dad. He just continued to pack up his books.

Dad stepped into the kitchen, looked around and saw we were packing up our school things. "What's this?" he asked.

"We finished our homework early because we have a serious question to ask you," I explained.

"Really?" he asked. "Okay, but let me look over your homework first. I want to make sure you didn't rush through things."

After Dad was satisfied we had done our best work, we stuffed everything in our backpacks, placed them by the front door, and headed back to the kitchen.

"How does roast beef sandwiches and chicken noodle soup sound for dinner?" Dad asked.

"Sounds good," I said. "The roast beef was really tender yesterday; it'll make good sandwiches. Don't forget the chili sauce!"

Dad grinned while he opened a couple cans of chicken noodle soup, poured them into a pot, and put it on the burner to slowly heat. Then he turned to us and asked, "Okay, what's going on? What's on your minds?"

"Well," I began, "we stopped by the chocolate shop after school today to get a little treat." I didn't mention ordering Dad's chocolates. "Of course, we stopped at home first and brought Neelia along. Georgina wasn't in a good mood. In fact, she yelled at Frankie to get 'that cat' out of her store."

"She yelled?" asked Dad.

"Well, maybe not yelled, but she wasn't pleasant about it," I answered.

"She serves food, you know. I've told you . . . you cannot take Neelia into every store. You have to respect the rules, and you know better than to take Neelia into a place that serves food."

"You're right, Dad," I said, "but that's not what we wanted to talk to you about. When Georgina yelled—I mean, firmly told us to take Neelia outside, Frankie picked her up and found this piece of paper in her mouth."

I handed him the letter I had attempted to straighten, complete with Neelia's teeth marks.

"Did you guys read this?" Dad asked.

"Yes," I said, with my head bowed. "I suppose that was wrong, too. I can't make out what it's saying, but I think it's really serious."

"Yes, it was wrong," said Dad. "But since the damage is done, let's see what it is and if it's why Georgina is so upset. Perhaps we can help."

Dad took time to look it over. All the while, he never had a good look on his face. After a bit, he simply got up from the table, stirred the soup, and got everything out of the refrigerator to make the sandwiches.

"What is it, Dad?" I asked. "Is it serious?"

"Yes, Ginni and Frankie, it's serious," Dad answered. "Mr. Snidely, Georgina's landlord, wants to evict her so he can take over her location. He's the landlord to the Walk and Talk Cellular store next door, too, and he wants to expand to build a cell phone megastore."

"What does 'evict' mean?" Frankie asked. He had been so quiet throughout all of this, I almost forgot he was sitting there.

"Evict means kick out. He said he wants her out by the end of the month. And since they have a year-by-year contract and the year is up, he can demand she leave," Dad explained.

"We can't lose the chocolate shop!" I cried. "Georgina has been grumpy lately, and I guess we now know why—but we can't let her lose her store!"

"What can we do?" asked Frankie.

Dad didn't answer right away, but I could see he thought about this while he made the sandwiches. He didn't sing his little ditties or tell his silly jokes like he did when he was in a good mood.

Without being told, I set the table. When Dad served the soup and sandwiches, he announced, "I think I have a plan."

Petition to Keep Sweet Georgina's Chocolate Shoppe

CHAPTER 5

THE PLAN

"What is it?" Frankie and I asked. "What's the plan?"

"Well," Dad started, "when citizens want to get their voices heard on a controversial decision, they often put together a petition and get lots of people to sign it. That way, the people who are deciding know what other people are thinking."

Frankie looked puzzled. Dad continued, "Let me explain. Frankie, you probably don't remember this because it happened several years ago, and you were too young, but Ginni, do you remember that the city council had wanted to demolish our local swimming pool rather than spending money on repairs?"

"Yes," I replied, "I vaguely remember that the pool might be closing."

"When the city council wanted to close the pool, many people in Makawee were not happy about it, including your mom and me. We wanted our children to learn to swim and enjoy summer fun in the pool. We also felt the pool was a benefit to the town and helped families decide to move to Makawee instead of a nearby town that didn't have a pool. So, a group of citizens talked with other citizens. If they agreed the pool should stay open, they signed their name on a piece of paper. This piece of paper is called a petition. So many people signed the petition that the city council kept the pool open even though it was expensive."

Dad continued, "I think this might work in this situation, too. If Mr. Snidely sees how important Sweet Georgina's Chocolate Shoppe is to the people of Makawee, he may realize closing it down could upset people and ultimately be bad for his cell phone business."

"Great," Frankie said, "let's get started!"

Then I thought for a moment. "Dad," I said, "we don't have time to go to every house in Makawee. Mr. Snidely wants to close the chocolate shop at the end of the month, and it's almost Valentine's Day."

"You're right, Ginni. I will find out how many signatures we need for the petition to be a good representation. I'll put together the wording for a petition tonight after you kids go to bed. Tomorrow we can talk to Georgina about it. We can't go around talking about her shop without her approving what we're doing. And the two of you have apologies to give her."

"Apologies?" I asked. "More than one?"

"Yes, one apology for bringing Neelia into the store and another for not immediately bringing back the piece of paper Neelia had in her mouth," Dad answered.

It hit me then. Of all the things Neelia could have taken from the store, she somehow took the one that could let us help Georgina and turn things around for her. Neelia was simply amazing!

"We have to go back?" Frankie pitifully asked. "She'll be even more mad at us."

"Yes," said Dad. "But when we talk to her about a petition, she may have some hope. And hope is a powerful thing. Maybe that'll even help lighten her mood. And believe me, while she was rightfully upset about your bringing Neelia into her store, what she really is upset about is losing her business. That's a terrible stress on anybody.

"Now the two of you get ready for bed, and I'll get started drafting the petition," Dad said, and he kissed us goodnight.

I walked Frankie and Neelia upstairs, and I could see that Frankie was still upset. "Don't worry," I told him. "Everyone makes mistakes, like we did taking Neelia inside Georgina's shop. She'll forgive us—especially when we tell her we're going to help."

"But she's been so grumpy lately," he whined.

"You heard what Dad said," I continued. "She's not all that mad at you, just like she wasn't really mad at that little girl who was ordering candy on Sunday. She's just really, really worried. And it'll feel good if we can help. Dad and I will be right by your side."

I brushed the top of his head as he headed to his bedroom. As he walked away, I heard him talking to Neelia.

"Did you hear that, little girl? It'll be okay. While Dad and Ginni take care of me, I'll take care of you."

But will we all be able to take care of Georgina? I wondered.

When I stepped into my room, there it was again—weird lights circling in the backyard while Tyto chased them. And once again, as soon as I turned on my light, the lights in the yard went off. Eerie!

CHAPTER 6

THE APOLOGY - BUT NOT THE EXPECTED ONE

The next day at school dragged on. I checked the clock frequently, and I was lucky if five minutes had gone by since the last time I checked. I was too excited and nervous to concentrate on schoolwork. I wanted to get the apology done and over with, but more importantly, I wanted to see if we could help Georgina.

When Catherine and I left school for the day, we waited for Frankie, Sharnelle, and Rose like usual. Frankie and Sharnelle came out the door, but Rose was not with them. Just then, I noticed Ms. Pebbles marching up the sidewalk. I wondered what was going on and hoped it wouldn't delay Frankie's and my getting home.

"What are you doing here, Mom?" asked Catherine.

"It seems your youngest sister got into a little situation today. I'm meeting with Ms. Nineon to get things settled. You all might as well come with me and sit outside the office while I have our talk and then I'll drive us all home."

When we got to Ms. Nineon's office, she came out and greeted Ms. Pebbles. She asked her and Rose, who had been sitting outside her office, to step inside.

Catherine and I exchanged a wondering look. What could Rose have done? Ms. Pebbles left Ms. Nineon's office door ajar, and Catherine, Sharnelle, Frankie, and I all heard the entire story.

"Thank you for coming in, Ms. Pebbles," Ms. Nineon started. "I know how busy you are at the hospital. I could have simply told you about the situation over the phone, but I wasn't comfortable sending Rose home with her Valentine's Day mailbox."

"Now you really have me curious, Ms. Nineon," said Ms. Pebbles. "What's wrong with Rose's Valentine's Day mailbox?"

Ms. Nineon picked up the box from the counter behind her desk. "Nothing is really wrong with the mailbox; it's actually a very cute design," she said. "It's a snake charmer basket, isn't it, Rose?"

Rose said nothing, just nodded her head.

"While I appreciate students who creatively go above and beyond, Rose added just a little too much realism to her Valentine's Day project. Rose, why don't you tell your mom in your own words what happened," instructed Ms. Nineon.

"I got the idea in January when Sharnelle and I went to Treehouse Crafts," began Rose. "They had a bunch of cardboard boxes there that you could decorate into all sorts of things. And then I saw this round box, and it was the perfect size for a snake charmer basket.

"Sharnelle bought it for me," Rose continued, "but I paid her back out of my allowance as soon as we got home. I took some rope that we had in the garage and glued it round and round the box and cover. I thought it turned out pretty cool."

"Yes," said Ms. Nineon. "It is a cute idea, and it turned out nicely. I can tell you put a lot of time into creating it. But that's not the end of the story, is it?"

"Well, what good is a snake charmer basket without a snake?" asked Rose.

Ms. Pebbles shook her head and said, "You didn't."

"She did," said Ms. Nineon. "A snake charmer basket, complete with a snake. And what I've been told is that when a little girl in her class opened the basket to place her valentine inside, she screamed, and everyone rushed over to see.

"As they were all pushing to get a look, the basket tipped over on the floor. The kids screamed. Many of them climbed on top of their desks, while several of the brave ones went running after the snake as it slithered away.

"Mrs. Jacobs, Rose's teacher, had to call Mr. Mike, the custodian, to the rescue. And thankfully, Mr. Mike saw the snake and captured it before it found its way into the ventilation system."

"Was it Sammy, your pet garter snake?" asked Ms. Pebbles.

Again, Rose said nothing but nodded her head.

"That poor thing must have been scared to death!" exclaimed Ms. Pebbles.

"That's one reason I called you in this afternoon," Ms. Nineon went on. "I think the little critter has had enough stress for one day, and I wanted to make sure it got home safely."

"What will be the consequences, Ms. Nineon?" asked Ms. Pebbles.

"Well, I've been thinking about that. There's nothing in the Principals' Guidebook that addresses snakes being brought to school in a Valentine's Day mailbox," she said with a little laugh. "But I believe missing a day of recess and helping Mr. Mike empty the classroom wastepaper baskets during that time would be best."

"Sounds good," said Ms. Pebbles. "And on our end, Rose, you will clean all of the critter cages at home. It'll take you more than one day after school, but you'll work on them until they are all done."

"All of them?" gasped Rose.

"Yes, all. And they will be cleaned to *my* standards. Thank you, Ms. Nineon, I'm glad you called. Now Rose, what do you have to say?"

"I'm sorry," said Rose.

"Sorry for what?" asked Ms. Pebbles. "It's not good enough to simply say sorry; you have to apologize for what you did wrong."

"I'm sorry I brought Sammy to school and caused a big mess in the classroom," said Rose.

"That's better," said Ms. Pebbles.

"You know, Rose," said Ms. Nineon, "you are welcome to bring your snake charmer basket back to school tomorrow—minus the snake, of course!"

"Thank you, Ms. Nineon," said Rose, "but I think I've had enough of Valentine's Day for one year."

"Are you sure?" asked Ms. Pebbles. "You'll miss getting treats along with the valentines."

"Yeah, I'm sure," said Rose. "I'm okay."

Ms. Pebbles stood up and shook Ms. Nineon's hand. Then Rose, Sammy in the Valentine's Day mailbox, and Ms. Pebbles came out of the office. Thankfully, the car ride home was a short one. No one said anything as we drove the few blocks back to our neighborhood.

"Thanks for the ride home," I called to Ms. Pebbles as Frankie and I got out of the car.

"Always nice to have your company," Ms. Pebbles said back to me. Then she turned and said, "Let's get Sammy settled. Rose, you can start cleaning while I start dinner."

As I walked home from the Pebbles', I thought, *Now it's Frankie's and my turn to say our apologies to Georgina.* I wondered what our consequences would be.

We both rushed into the house and ran upstairs to change our clothes. I also wanted to give Mr. Whiskers his afternoon snack. Frankie beat me upstairs, and when he walked into his bedroom, I told him to hurry and get ready.

I had to smile as I walked farther down the hall to my bedroom. I noticed when I passed Frankie's room that he had been working on his origami, and I could tell he was making a mouse. I went over to Mr. Whiskers' cage, picked him up and said, "He'd better add really long whiskers to his origami mouse like you have, my friend."

Mr. Whiskers answered by wiggling his nose.

"I wish I could take you along, little guy, but if Georgina got upset with a kitten in her store, imagine what she would do if she caught you!" I snuggled Mr. Whiskers again before changing into sweats and a sweatshirt.

"Frankie," I called as I left my bedroom, "let's get our homework done early again."

Frankie got to our curved staircase before I did, and he and Neelia went bumpity-bump down the stairs. I giggled as I watched them. Whenever they did this, it looked as if Neelia was laughing right along with Frankie. After Mom died, Frankie didn't bumpity-bump down the stairs again until Neelia joined our home. I was glad to see him acting more like himself again.

Like yesterday, we were done with our homework when Dad announced he was home.

"Hi, Dad," I said as he walked into the kitchen.

"Hi, kids. We've a lot to do this afternoon, and I didn't want to hold up Georgina, so I came home early. And as luck would have it, my last patient had to cancel his appointment because he has the flu," Dad said.

"This is getting to be a good routine," he commented before he looked at our schoolwork. After we again passed the homework check, the three of us sat down at the table, and Dad shared with us what he had accomplished that day.

"Do you guys remember my friend Jeff Ace?" asked Dad. "He's the lead attorney at Ace Legal. He had some free time over lunch today, so we discussed Georgina's situation.

"He first said that since Georgina was in a year-to-year contract, the landlord has every right to end the lease when the year is up. But he liked the idea of trying to persuade Mr. Snidely, her landlord, that closing the chocolate shop may not be in his best business interest. With approximately 15,000 people in town, he said that 2,070 signatures would be sufficient to represent the citizens' opinions. And of course, the more the better. He helped me put the words together and come up with how to explain the situation to people when asking for their signatures.

"So, I guess we are ready to head over to the chocolate shop, make our apologies, and see what Georgina has to say about a petition," Dad concluded.

"I guess Neelia should stay home on this trip, huh, Dad?" Frankie asked.

Dad laughed and agreed. "That would be best, Frankie. However, Neelia found the notice. So, if Georgina agrees with all of this, she might see Neelia in a different light."

Neelia

CHAPTER 7

THE EXPECTED APOLOGY

It seemed odd to be walking downtown without Neelia. When we left the house, I saw her peering out the window and watching us walk away. She's not used to being left behind, either.

"Do you guys hear that?" questioned Dad.

"The whirring noise?" I asked back.

Dad replied, "Yes, I've noticed that sound a couple of other times as well, but I can't tell where it's coming from."

Yes! Someone else has heard the noise, too—I'm not paranoid, I thought to myself. I said, "I've been hearing it for a while, but I don't know what's making it either." I debated with myself if I should also tell Dad about the strange lights I'd been seeing in the backyard, but before I could decide, we were at Sweet Georgina's Chocolate Shoppe.

Luckily, no one was shopping when we stepped inside. I didn't want to have to apologize in front of people, that's for sure!

"Well, Jim," Georgina greeted Dad, "how can I help you today? I was just about to make myself a cup of Earl Grey tea. Would you like one?" Although she wasn't sharp with Dad the way she had been with Frankie and me, she was still not her cheery, smiling self.

"I'll pass on the tea today, thanks, but my children have something they'd like to tell you, Georgina, if you have a minute," Dad said.

"I do," Georgina replied curtly.

I thought it best for Frankie if I began. "Georgina, Frankie and I are both really sorry for the other day. We know better than to bring Neelia into a store that serves food. It's just that Neelia is so much a part of the family that sometimes I think we forget she's a cat," I said with a slight smile. Georgina didn't smile back.

"But we have more to apologize for," I continued. (Ms. Pebbles would have been pleased with my remembering not only to apologize, but to say what I was apologizing for.) "When Frankie picked up Neelia and we went outside, he didn't realize that Neelia had a wad of paper in her mouth. We were both shaken when we left your store, so we took the piece of paper home and showed it to Dad instead of bringing it back to you."

Dad interjected, "Frankie, what do you have to say for yourself?"

"I'm really sorry," Frankie whispered. I leaned down to his ear and softly told Frankie to tell Georgina what he was sorry about.

"I'm sorry I brought Neelia into your store," Frankie continued. "I just love her so much; I can't imagine anyone not wanting Neelia around. But I will be more careful—especially in places that serve food."

I saw Georgina's mood soften. Like Neelia, Frankie's innocence had a way of touching hearts.

"As long as you both remember not to bring any of your pets into my store in the future, apology accepted. But what piece of paper did Neelia find?"

Dad took over at this point. "Georgina, again, my children know better than not to have returned this to you immediately, but in this case, I'm glad that it turned out the way it did. Neelia found your eviction notice from Mr. Snidely."

As soon as Dad said this, I saw Georgina's face fall and tears immediately come to the corners of her eyes.

Dad reached out his hand, took one of Georgina's hands in his, and with his other hand, gently lifted her face so that he could look her directly in the eye. "I think we can help you," he kindly said.

Georgina couldn't hold it in any longer. She broke down and sobbed and laid her head on Dad's shoulder as Dad patted her on her back to comfort her. He let her cry it out until at last Georgina broke from Dad's hug and went to get a tissue.

She then came over to us, bent down, and said, "I'm truly sorry for being so short with you the other day. Let's all sit down in my back office and see what your dad is suggesting."

After we crowded into her small back office, Dad explained the petition. He told her we would organize the petition and get as many people to sign it as possible. I thought Georgina was going to cry all over again.

"Do you really think this will work?" she asked.

"We won't know until we try," Dad replied. "But since legally you have no way to stop the eviction, we have to try a different route. I've dealt with Mr. Snidely before, and I don't think that he'll decide to cancel the eviction just to be a nice guy. We have to hit him where it hurts—in his pocketbook. If we can convince him he'll lose money by making enough people angry that he's closed a beloved store, that *might* give him second thoughts. In my opinion, it's the only option we have, and it's certainly worth a shot!"

That was all it took for Georgina, and she started to cry again, so Frankie and I disappeared to check out the candy counters. It didn't take as long this time before Georgina composed herself. In a few moments, Dad and Georgina stepped out of the office.

"Well, Georgina," Dad said, "It's time for us to get busy. Jeff at Ace Legal helped me draft up the petition, and I think sending the kids out with Neelia will have the greatest impact."

"I can't thank you enough, Jim," said Georgina. "Even if we don't convince Mr. Snidely, just knowing that I have people who care about me and my shop makes me feel so much better."

After saying this, Georgina stepped over to us and gave us a great big hug. Frankie was wide-eyed as she held us tight, and it felt really weird. Right after the hug, she went behind the counter and picked out a Sea Salt Dark Chocolate Caramel and a Peppermint Buttercreme and gave them to Frankie and me.

"Thank you," we both said in amazement.

First Georgina's grumpy with everyone, including Frankie and me, and now she was hugging us and giving us chocolates like we're best friends. Adults! Geesh! Who could keep up?

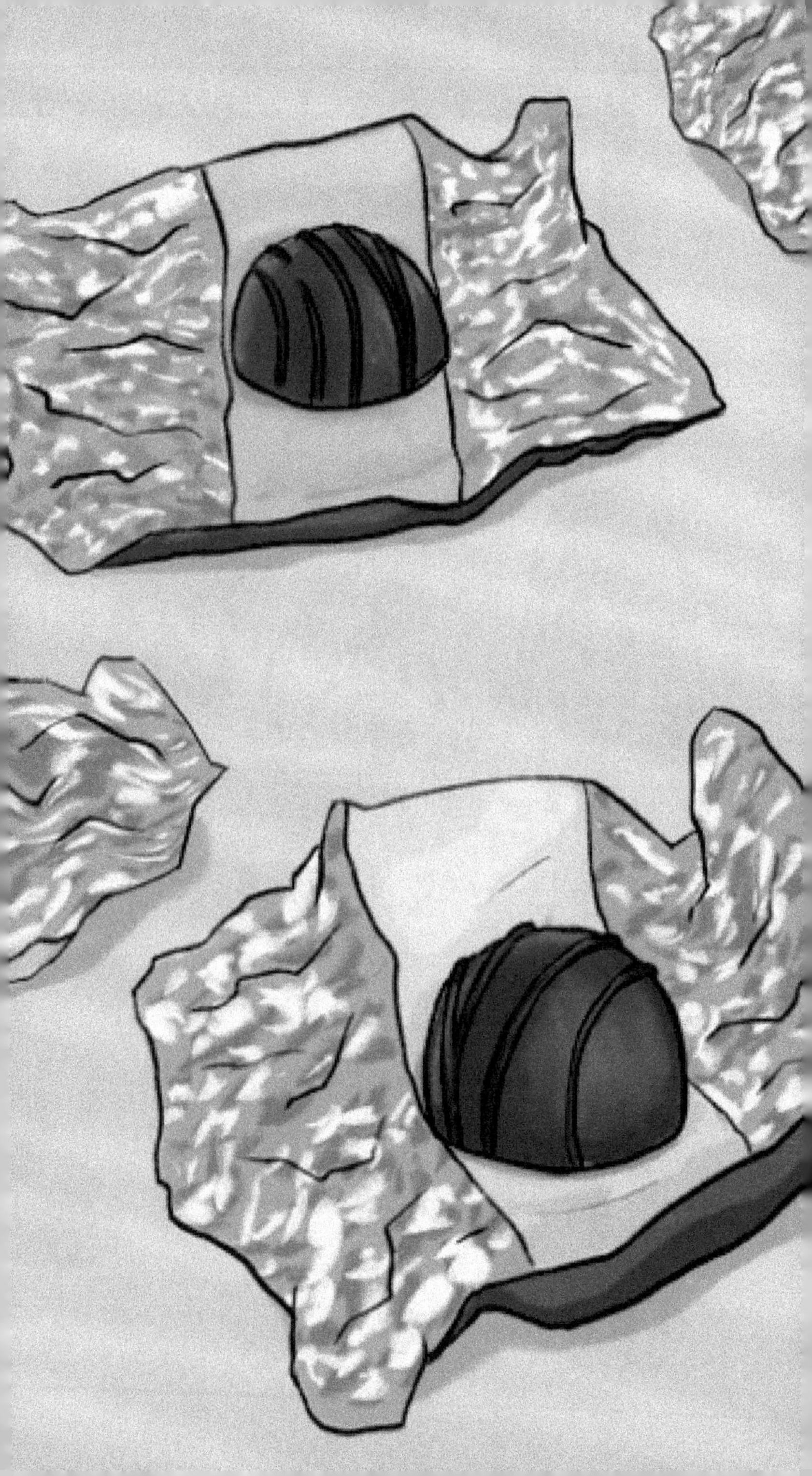

CHAPTER 8

THE PETITION BEGINS

The other day when school dragged on was nothing like how it dragged on Petition Day. Time even crawled during art, one of my favorite classes. I touched base with Frankie during noon recess, and the first thing he said was, "Will this school day ever end?"

Finally, the last bell rang. Catherine knew how anxious I was to get going and told me not to wait for her and her sisters. She was always so good at reading situations and helping. So, I grabbed Frankie, one of the first kids out the door, and we raced home.

Frankie and I decided that we should leave our school clothes on rather than change into sweats. All we had to do was drop off our backpacks, grab Neelia, and head toward Pearly White Dentistry. I had a last-minute thought while Frankie harnessed Neelia. I went upstairs to my room and asked Mr. Whiskers if he wanted to ride along, tucked unseen in my scarf. His eyes got big, and I could swear he nodded his head. I grabbed a scrap of fabric from my sewing table and quickly sewed it to the underside of my scarf. This would keep him out of sight. I went back downstairs and told Frankie that Mr. Whiskers was riding along, too. Neelia leaned on my arm and sniffed until Mr. Whiskers poked his head out, and they nuzzled.

Dad had arranged his schedule so he would be available to talk to us as soon as we arrived. "Here's the petition on a clipboard, several pens, and an index card with what to say when people answer the door. Let me hear you practice it several times before you head out," Dad instructed.

Knowing that I'd be doing all the talking, I cleared my throat and read from the card:

Thank you for coming to the door.

My name is Ginni, and this is my brother, Frankie, and our cat Neelia. We won't take much of your time, but have you heard that Sweet Georgina's Chocolate Shoppe is closing by the end of February? She's losing her lease. We want to show her landlord that we love her store and ask him to reconsider and let her stay.

Would you please sign this petition to acknowledge that you, too, would like the store to stay open?

I practiced it with Dad umpteen times until he said I was ready to go. "Once you've read this repeatedly, Ginni, you'll be able to say it without the index card. Before you go, however, there are some safety rules you must follow.

"As always, be careful crossing streets. I know you're old enough to not have to be reminded of this, but you'll have a lot on your mind, and you can't forget basic safety. Also, never go into anyone's home. If they won't sign it while you're at the front door, just walk away.

"I went by We Love Pets today and bought a traveling cat water container. I have that and two bottles of water for the two of you to put into this small backpack I bought. You may not need it on your after-school trips, but you might this weekend when you're out longer.

"If anything happens that you're not comfortable with, like someone making fun of the situation or saying mean things, just walk away. I rarely have my cell phone on while I'm in the office, but I will while you and Frankie are out. Call me if you need anything.

"Also, I arranged with Bonnie, Dr. Little's receptionist, to drive you. She's been home for a couple of weeks recovering from minor surgery, and she's really bored. Bonnie is more than willing to stay in her car and follow you kids to make sure everything goes okay. She will also bring you home when you are done for the afternoon. Be home before dark, and I'll have supper ready for you."

Then Dad flipped the card over. It had the list of safety rules on it. Dad had also given us a map and had divided the town into different zones. That way, we could concentrate on one neighborhood at a time. After we both agreed that we would be extra cautious while out, I loaded up the backpack, met Bonnie outside, and we were off.

I wasn't at all surprised when I looked up and saw Tyto circling overhead. I had a feeling that he, too, would be part of our petitioning party. I waved, and he tilted one of his wings toward me.

Bonnie drove a couple of blocks south of downtown to begin. I must admit, I was pretty nervous. When we were out of the car, I heard that nagging whirring sound and that didn't help at all.

"I hear the sound that you and Dad mentioned you've been hearing," Frankie said as we were walking to our first house. "I don't like it but it doesn't seem to bother Neelia." As if to agree with Frankie, Neelia let out a small meow.

"I don't like it either, Frankie, but I don't know what to do about it," I told him. "We've too much to do to let it bother us, so let's just concentrate on our mission."

"Okay," was all Frankie said. He and Neelia continued to cuddle as we walked to the first door.

Easier for me to say than to do, I thought. But I stopped thinking about it as soon as I knocked on door number one.

I had to giggle when I saw who answered the door. It was Jeanie Hops, one of Dad's part-time dental hygienists and one of Mom's best friends. That's why Dad had us start here—with an easy one!

Jeanie was very nice as she listened to my speech (after so many practices with Dad, I didn't need to read it word-for-word from the card).

"Of course, I want to keep the chocolate shop!" she said. "Where do I sign?" I handed her the clipboard, and we had our first signature.

I wish I could say that they were all as easy as Jeanie, but that, of course, wasn't to be. The biggest struggle we had was finding people at home. On my map, I circled the houses where no one answered just in case we had time to go back and knock on the door again.

It didn't take too long before a pattern emerged. I'd knock on the door, the person would peer outside, and if they opened their door and listened to my speech, we had a chance. I'd like to say that I had strong powers of persuasion, but I know better.

Sometimes after I finished my speech, the person would say something like:

. . . I don't want to get involved, or

. . . I don't sign petitions, or

. . . No, thank you.

But if they glanced down at Frankie holding Neelia, then they almost always signed. This happened over and over again. One look into Neelia's big green eyes and a small cooing meow was all it took. They'd look at her and ask me where to sign. I'd place the clipboard in their hand, and they'd quickly glance at the line where they were to sign while they kept gazing at Neelia.

We were just about done for the afternoon and the sun was slowing sinking into the horizon when we made our last stop. I knocked as usual and froze when I saw who opened the door. Standing there in all his splendor was Mr. Smiley, the used car salesperson. I had seen him on TV commercials since I was a little kid. "You'll smile too when you drive off in a car from Smiley's Auto World," he'd say at the end of every commercial.

I had never talked to anyone who had been on TV before. Frankie had to poke me in the ribs to get me to start my speech. This time, I needed to read the card from beginning to end. I didn't trust my memory when I was in front of a celebrity.

He was just about to brush us off when Neelia meowed. Mr. Smiley looked down at her and got a glazed look in his eyes. "Where do I sign?" was all he said.

I thanked him and as we walked away, I heard him mutter, "Just what happened? I never sign petitions. What got over me?"

I texted Dad and said we were done for the day and Bonnie would bring us home.

"I can't believe how many signatures you got on your first time out," Dad exclaimed as he looked over the signed sheets.

"We'd have gotten more if more people would have been home," Frankie added.

"Nevertheless, that's a wonderful beginning. You have over thirty signatures!" Dad said. "The staff and I were talking in the office, and we put a petition on the counter with a copy of the index card in case people choose to read it and sign it while they're in my office. I have five more to add to the list. I think we should celebrate with a burger and nuggets at the Village Diner tonight. How does that sound?"

"Yahoo!" we both cried.

Before we left the house, I picked up Neelia and whispered in her ear, "I don't know how you did it, little girl, but thank you for convincing so many people to sign the petition. You are a marvel, and we all love you so very much." With that, I kissed the side of her face and got the sweetest meow in return. I had to brush away a few happy tears from my cheeks as I crawled into the car with Dad and Frankie.

My burger never tasted so good.

CHAPTER 9

WHAT'S THIS?

The next day at school was easier to handle. We had made a plan, and the plan was working. I concentrated on schoolwork, which was a good thing since I had been distracted these past few days and I was behind.

When we went to lunch, the entire class was surprised to see a small table set aside in the hallway with a special Valentine Day's mailbox on it. "What's this, I wonder?" asked Ms. Zinger. She read the small sign to the class as we crowded around the display.

"This Valentine's Day mailbox is something new," Ms. Zinger said. "If you don't know, boys and girls, leukemia and lymphoma are a certain type of cancer that often targets children."

I heard someone from the back of the class shout out, "This is a great idea."

"I agree. Let's talk about this as a class after lunch," Ms. Zinger said as she marched us down to the cafeteria.

When Catherine and I had a private moment at recess, she told me, "I wonder if this has anything to do with Sharnelle's classmate. Sharnelle came home one day saying that Katie Lansing would not be in school for a long time because she is fighting cancer."

"Sure could," I agreed. "But I wonder who set this up?"

Attention

During this month of showing and sharing love, please consider giving a small donation to help the Leukemia and Lymphoma society. People who are fighting for their lives need your

Love

more than ever

When we got back inside after recess, Ms. Zinger told us she had an important announcement. "Boys and girls," she said, "the teachers and I talked about the special Valentine's Day mailbox that is in the hallway while we ate our lunch today. Ms. Nineon stepped in as well. We all agreed that this is something we should support. But we thought we'd have a little fun with it. All the classrooms will take a special collection in their rooms rather than put anything in the mailbox in the hallway. Then at the assembly, when we pass out the awards for the best Valentine's Day mailboxes, we will see which classroom contributed the most to the Leukemia and Lymphoma Society. The classroom with the biggest collection will earn a pizza party."

"Yeah!" the class shouted in unison.

"But who made the mailbox in the hallway?" someone asked.

"That's quite a puzzle," Ms. Zinger acknowledged. "It seems none of the teachers, and not even Ms. Nineon, knows anything about it. But we decided that even though we don't know the source, it is a good idea for a good cause."

Stanley started shouting, "Pizza, pizza, pizza . . ." and the entire class joined in. Ms. Zinger laughed before she waved her hands to get us to calm down.

"Okay, with that settled, let's move on to our math lesson," Ms. Zinger stated.

With only a few groans, we all pulled out our math books, and the school day continued.

Just like the previous day, Frankie and I scooted

home, dropped off our books, grabbed Neelia and Mr. Whiskers, and headed out with the petitions in hand with Tyto following overhead. Zone 2 was our neighborhood. Since I knew that Ms. Pebbles wouldn't be home from work, we skipped her house, turned the corner, and showed up on Mr. Steve's doorstep.

Mr. Steve is a very nice older guy who loves to bake brownies. The neighbors are often the willing recipients of his chocolate treats. I remember that Mom, too, had loved his brownies. When Mr. Steve got to the door, I was surprised to see a young boy shyly peeping out from behind him while he pleasantly greeted us.

I thought it best to get right to my index card rather than ask about the boy—business first.

"Of course, I want to keep the chocolate shop!" Mr. Steve exclaimed after my speech. "That's where I get the special cocoa for my brownies. Where do I sign?"

After the petition was signed, I didn't have to be nosy and ask about the boy, because Mr. Steve volunteered the information.

"Now that business is out of the way, I'd like you to meet my grandson, Scott," Mr. Steve said. Scott was still standing behind his grandpa, so Mr. Steve gently pulled him forward. "Scott is going to be staying with me for a fairly long time. Long enough, in fact, that I'm going in tomorrow to get him registered for first grade so he can start school on Monday."

"Great!" Frankie exclaimed. "He'll be in my grade! It'll be fun to have another boy my age in the neighborhood."

"Say," I said, "why don't you ask that Scott be placed in Mrs. Jacobs' class with Frankie? That way, when he starts, he'll already have a friend."

"Excellent suggestion, Ginni," said Mr. Steve. "I'll do just that."

"I hope you get into my classroom, Scott. I'll introduce you to my friends. At noon we always have a game of dodgeball going. You like dodgeball?" Frankie prattled.

After a moment, Scott quietly said, "I do."

"Well, we'd best get going. We have a lot of doors to knock on this afternoon," I said.

"See you Monday!" Frankie said as he waved goodbye to Scott. Scott nodded and looked down at his feet.

I was glad that a boy Frankie's age had moved into the neighborhood. Friends are a great thing. I looked down at Frankie and said, "Hmm. He was awfully quiet, don't you think?"

Frankie replied, "Yeah. He seemed really shy."

"I wonder why he's staying with his grandfather for so long. That seems kinda strange," I continued. "You will have to help him make friends, Frankie." Frankie nodded as we went on our way.

After many more doors and more signatures, we had finished for the afternoon. Bonnie dropped us off just as Dad came home.

Dad said, "Sorry I'm home late. With all the work on the petition lately, I got behind on my billing. How did you two fare?"

"Almost everyone who was home signed the petition

once they looked at Neelia's cute face," I said. Dad was impressed when he saw the number of signatures on the petition sheets.

"I have some good news as well," he announced. "Seems like the word about the petition has already spread. It started when Irving at Handyman's Hardware stopped in to ask me about it. He loves Sweet Georgina's Chocolate Shoppe, and he asked if he could have a petition at his store for people to sign there as well. After that, four or five other business owners came in to get copies. I think this just might work!"

Dad put a frozen pizza in the oven for a quick and easy dinner. For a frozen pizza, it was pretty tasty. It wasn't long before Frankie and I eagerly headed to bed. I don't know if it was all the fresh air after school or the emotions of everything going on, but I was exhausted and was in bed about a half hour before my normal bedtime.

As I was getting comfortable for the night, I rolled over, faced the window, and saw the strange lights appear. *Ha, ha*, I said to myself. *I fooled you by going to bed early.* I lay there and watched the light sweep back and forth along the backyard. Tyto was out there, too—again chasing the light. This lasted for about thirty minutes before the light finally winked out. I imagined Tyto went back to his maple tree perch as I lay there thinking.

I thought I should be scared about the backyard lights and the whirring sounds that followed me outside, but there was something inside me that wouldn't let me get overly concerned. Neelia hadn't been concerned about it, either. I was more curious than anything else. As I twirled my hair, I went to sleep, mentally making a list of everything it could be. But I must admit, my list wasn't very long.

CHAPTER 10

VALENTINE'S DAY

The following week went along much as the previous week had. I did my best to keep up with everything at school so that I could spend as much time as possible with the petitions. And they were everywhere! There were copies at Yummy Tummy, Dr. Little's Veterinarian Clinic, Treehouse Crafts, the Village Diner, and almost every other store in town. Plus, people made yard signs that said "Save Sweet Georgina's Chocolate Shoppe" and displayed them on stakes pounded into the frozen ground in their front yards. *This has to work,* I said to myself over and over.

All of a sudden, I got a flashback to last Christmas break when we were worrying whether or not we'd be able to keep Neelia. I clearly saw in my mind Dad and I standing in the kitchen and Dad telling me how important it was to "believe." Just a couple of months later, we were again in a "believe" situation. I decided to take Dad's advice again and believe that we'd be able to help Georgina save her shop.

But now it was Friday, Valentine's Day. The day dragged on with everyone eager for the two o'clock assembly. We were all more excited than usual, for not only were we going to see who won the Best Mailbox Award for every classroom, but we'd also find out which classroom would be honored with a pizza party for the Leukemia and Lymphoma collection. Frankie and I both had contributed two weeks' worth of allowance money to our classroom mailboxes.

Finally, Ms. Nineon got on the intercom and called us down to the gymnasium. She always called the older grades first because we sat at the top of the bleachers since we could easily see over the little kids who sat in front. When the gymnasium was full, Ms. Nineon got the assembly started by talking to us about why we celebrate Valentine's Day at school. Is it for the contest? Is it to see who gets the most valentines? Is it for the candy? Or is it to remind us to be kind to one another? Whenever Ms. Nineon talks to us at these assemblies about how to treat each other, I sure wish Stanley would take her message to heart.

The awards were given away as usual. Neither Frankie nor I won Best Mailbox for our classrooms, but I'm happy to say that Catherine's "Pets' Favorite Vet Clinic" won in her room. I wasn't surprised, and I was thrilled for her. When her name was called, I stood up, clapped, and cheered. I got some strange looks from kids around me, but I didn't care—I supported my friend.

The classroom winners stood in front and held their trophies while the newspaper guy positioned himself to take pictures. Suddenly Mr. Mike, the custodian, walked up front and stood next to them.

Everyone in the school knows Mr. Mike, but we had never seen him go onstage at an assembly before. Even Ms. Nineon was obviously taken aback when Mr. Mike walked to her and asked her for the microphone.

“Of course,” she said, and she handed him the cordless mic as she stepped aside.

“Boys and girls,” began Mr. Mike, “I have a little story to tell you. Every year we have this contest, and every year one boy or girl in each classroom wins a little trophy and all of you get to take home a bunch of Valentines, many with candy. But this year, because of an innocent oversight, one little girl gave up her valentines for the year.”

As soon as Mr. Mike said that, I knew he was taking about Rose! I immediately looked at Catherine, who at first looked down but then held her head up high to support her sister. Where was he going with this? Hadn’t Rose been punished enough? Even Ms. Nineon had a quizzical look on her face.

“This little girl,” Mr. Mike continued, “came to me during her recess to help me empty the classroom wastebaskets, as so many boys and girls have done in the past when they’ve made a mistake. Some kids grumble and are upset about losing recess, and some of them couldn’t care less and continue to make poor choices throughout the year. But no other kid has ever come to me and said, ‘What more can I do to help make things right, Mr. Mike?’

“This girl knew about a child in her older sister’s grade who is not in school because she is in the hospital fighting cancer. She showed me a picture of Katie Lansing dressed in a cute pixie fairy costume. She asked if there was something we could do. That’s why the Valentine’s Day mailbox showed up in the hallway.

This girl and I are both so proud of this school that they took our small intention and turned it into a major school-wide fundraiser. That goes to show all of you, and all of us, just how special this school is.

"What Ms. Nineon doesn't know is that Katie's parents are here to thank all of us at Makawee Elementary on behalf of the Leukemia and Lymphoma Society. Ms. Nineon, is it okay for the parents to come forward now?"

Stunned, Ms. Nineon just nodded her head. The back doors opened, and Mr. and Mrs. Lansing walked into the gymnasium. By now, there was hardly a dry eye in the audience as we saw Mr. and Mrs. Lansing go stand by Mr. Mike.

Mr. Mike said, "Rose Pebbles, will you come forward, please?" Rose quietly got up from her seat on the bleachers, crawled around the kids who were next to her, and walked over to stand next to Mr. Mike.

Mr. Mike continued, "Mr. and Mrs. Lansing, I'm so proud of Rose, as I know you must be as well. With Ms. Nineon's permission, I would like Rose to present you with this check for the Leukemia and Lymphoma Society in Katie's honor."

Ms. Nineon nodded her head at Mr. Mike, and he handed Rose the check and asked her if she could read the amount. Rose got a scared look in her eyes, and Mr. Mike leaned down to her and whispered in her ear. He then turned to the audience and said, "I'm sure the Society will appreciate this check for . . ." and then he put the mic in front of Rose, who said, "3,542 dollars and 12 cents."

The gym erupted in mad applause. We had done fundraisers before, but we had never raised so much money. And to think it was all because of Rose, who had brought Sammy, her pet snake, to school!

When the applause died down, Rose started to walk back to her seat, but not before Mr. and Mrs. Lansing grabbed her and gave her a great big hug. That gave Catherine the courage to get out of the trophy line and go to her little sister as well. Right after that, Sharnelle left her seat on the bleachers and went to join them both. I was totally surprised when I looked down and saw Ms. Pebbles, with tears streaming down her face, walk out onto the floor and pick up Rose and hug her tight. Applause erupted again.

Ms. Nineon, trying to compose herself and regain control of the assembly, had to ask many times for quiet. She ended the assembly by giving us two messages. "Boys and girls, see what can happen when you make a mistake? All is not lost. You can come out stronger and better by learning from your mistake and doing something that helps to make the world a better place. In addition, look at what can happen when we all work together. What started out as a simple idea brought significant money to a worthwhile cause. Rose, thank you for demonstrating both of these lessons to us." And she, too, gave Rose a great big hug.

"And here is something else you need to always remember," she continued. "You can never tell just how or when you'll be rewarded with your good deeds. The folks at Yummy Tummy Groceries heard about our little contest and how well we were doing. To thank you all for your efforts, their deli is going to supply the pizza for pizza parties . . . for the entire school!"

Stanley again started the "pizza, pizza, pizza" chant, but this time he got the entire school to shout along. Normally Ms. Nineon wouldn't have been as forgiving about this as Ms. Zinger had been, but she smiled and let the chant die down.

"Now, the bus drivers are surely wondering where we are. We are long overdue for dismissal. Can I ask each of the teachers to lead their classrooms out for the day? Boys and girls, please be extra kind today and board the buses in an orderly fashion. We don't want to worry your parents by being later than we already are."

As the gym was emptying, Frankie and I went down to the floor and stood beside Ms. Pebbles and the girls, not wanting to leave without them. After the photographer took pictures of the trophy winners and of Rose with the Lansings, Frankie and I went to congratulate Rose. Ms. Pebbles gave us hugs as well, as if we were part of the family. She'll never know how much that meant to me.

Ms. Nineon walked the Pebbles family out the door and asked Ms. Pebbles how she had known to attend the assembly. She reported she got the strangest call from Mr. Mike the custodian saying that he couldn't tell her details, but that she would surely want to attend the assembly. "And, boy," said Ms. Pebbles, "I'm so glad I did. Say, where is Mr. Mike?" she asked. "I'd like to thank him for thinking to alert me."

"Now that you mention it," Ms. Nineon commented, "I haven't seen him since the presentation of the check. Isn't that just like him to do his job but stay out of the limelight? I will tell him just how much it meant to you to be here."

And with that, we all headed home. I couldn't wait to tell Dad what had happened at school. I knew he, too, would be proud of Rose.

After dinner that night, I ran upstairs right when we were done with dishes and grabbed the specially wrapped Valentine's Day gift box for Dad that I had been hiding under my bed. Bonnie had stopped at the chocolate shop when we were done with the petitions yesterday so that I could pick up Dad's Mint Meltaways.

Frankie and I each grabbed a side of the heart-shaped box and brought it to Dad as he was sitting in his recliner with Neelia on his lap.

"We love you," we said in unison as we gave him the box.

As soon as Dad opened it, he exclaimed, "You remembered my favorite! I haven't had a Mint Meltaway since the last batch your mom gave me." He reached his arms up to us, and we leaned in for a family hug. My cheek was damp as we straightened up from the embrace. Good to know that even Dad can still tear up when remembering Mom.

"And," he laughingly said as he pulled two gift boxes out from beside his recliner, "these are for the two best kids a dad could have." We giggled, too, when we saw two heart-shaped boxes from Georgina's. I guess we all had the same idea.

"You remembered, too," I laughed as we opened our boxes. Frankie's was filled with his favorite Peppermint Buttercremes, and mine held Sea Salt Dark Chocolate Covered Caramels.

CHAPTER 11

FIRST A CULPRIT, THEN A HERO

It was a week after the assembly, and Frankie and I were still hard at work collecting signatures. By now, the town was all abuzz about the chocolate shop. I often no longer had to explain the situation and go through my speech. Instead, people usually commented, "I was wondering when you would get here! Where do I sign?"

As we walked between houses, I asked Frankie how Scott was fitting in. Frankie had little to say other than he had indeed been placed in his classroom.

"He's doing okay now, I guess," said Frankie. "He's still quiet. I sometimes think that there's something seriously wrong going on. He seems so sad a lot of the time."

Leave it to my little brother to be sensitive to a new student. "Well," I said, "he is living with his grandfather for the time being. Something has to be going on with his parents. Scott will probably share with you when or if he's ever ready."

We had more than the 2,070 signatures Mr. Ace had suggested we get—so many more, in fact, that I had lost count. Whenever the sheet on the clipboard was full of signatures, we dropped it in a special basket we had set aside in the garage. Both Frankie and I were getting hungry, so Bonnie drove us back to our house where we could get a quick snack and pick up more blank petition pages. Bonnie said she was going to go to Yummy Tummy for a few groceries and would be right back.

When we got inside, Mr. Whiskers wiggled to get out, so I put him in an empty box that lay next to the recycling pile.

As we sat at the kitchen table and munched on Dad's homemade trail mix, we started to hear banging in the garage.

I should have been scared, but my curiosity took over. Frankie peered out from behind me while I opened the back door into the garage. I was startled and amused at the same time; there was Stanley in serious distress.

I couldn't tell at first what was going on, but he was dancing around as if he had ants in his pants. He had accidentally stepped into a bucket, and it was caught on his foot. It clanged as he jumped around. Meanwhile he was clutching a broom in one hand and slapping himself with it.

I started to belly laugh until I saw his unzipped backpack with pages of the petition sticking out.

"What are you doing?" I yelled at him as I turned on the light.

Startled, Stanley turned around in wide-eyed horror. "Get this mouse off of me!" he screamed.

It was then that I saw Mr. Whiskers crawl up Stanley's back, over his head, and down inside his shirt collar. Right after that, he sneaked out of Stanley's pant leg and ran into the house.

"He's gone," I curtly said. "Now, do you mind telling me what you're doing here and why you have our petitions in your backpack?"

As I said this, I was grateful to see Dad walking up the driveway. Bonnie was behind him in her car. She stepped out, surveyed the situation, and, with a smile on her face, said, "Looks like you guys are going to be busy for a while. I'll pick the kids up tomorrow." She got back into her car and drove away.

Stanley stood there not saying anything, just brushing himself off as if Mr. Whiskers was still running up and down his back.

"What's going on?" Dad asked as he stepped into the garage.

"I'd like to know myself," I said. "We just caught Stanley in the garage."

That's when I saw it. A drone was leaning against the workbench.

"That's it!" I yelled.

Stanley, Dad, and Frankie (who had been holding Neelia all this time) jumped.

"Look, Dad," I exclaimed. "A drone! That's what we've been hearing whirring around us for weeks. And I bet it has a light, and that's what I've been seeing in the backyard, too—isn't it, Stanley?"

Neelia meowed loudly as if to say, *See, I told you not to worry. It was just Stanley.*

"I think we had all better go inside and get this settled," Dad calmly said.

As Dad ushered us into the living room, I saw him take his phone out of his pocket. He stepped into his office, and he told all of us to sit down in the living room.

Before I sat down, I ran upstairs to check on Mr. Whiskers. There he was, running on his wheel as if nothing had happened. I reached into his cage since the door was still wide open, and he leapt into my hand. As I pulled him close to my face, I thanked him for catching Stanley in the act. Like before, he just wiggled his nose and nuzzled my neck in response. Among Neelia, Mr. Whiskers, and Tyto, it sure felt like we had some guardian angels on our side. As I gave him a little pat on the head and put him back in his cage, I glanced at my shelf where I had family photos on display. My eye caught the one of my mom's uncle holding me as a toddler. Uncle Butch was my mom's favorite uncle. He had lived in Makawee his whole life. He used to tickle me on my cheeks and neck with his extra-long moustache. I giggled at the memory, looked at Mr. Whiskers, and thought, "Hmmm . . . extra-long whiskers . . . I wonder." But I was needed downstairs. I closed Mr. Whiskers' cage and headed downstairs to join Frankie and Stanley.

We soon heard a knock on the door, and Dad went to open it. It was Stanley's dad.

"Thanks, Myron, for coming over," Dad said. "I think we have a great deal to discuss this afternoon."

Dad told Stanley's dad about the whirring sounds we'd been hearing when we walked around town. And since I had never told Dad about the backyard lights, he made me report that situation as well. Dad then said, "And most importantly, I'm very curious about the signed petitions we saw in Stanley's backpack."

"Son, what do you have to say for yourself?" his dad asked.

"I don't know," Stanley said with his head bowed. "I was just having a bit of fun with the drone you gave me for Christmas."

"Well, I don't think you'll be using that drone again anytime soon. Now, how about those petitions?" Stanley's dad asked. "What were you going to do with them?"

"Do I have to tell?" whispered Stanley.

One stern look from his dad was all it took for Stanley to admit his plan.

I couldn't believe the story that he shared. I didn't know that Stanley could be this devious. Most of his bluster was gone, however, as he told us his plan.

"All anyone is talking about these days is saving the chocolate shop. And whose names are always mentioned at the same time? All I keep hearing is, 'Aren't Ginni and Frankie doing such a marvelous job?' And 'Georgina will owe her store to them if she keeps it,' blah blah blah. I thought that if I took a batch of the signed petitions, I could bring them in, too, and I'd get some credit as well."

We were all silent for a long minute as what Stanley said sank in.

Dad broke the silence by saying, "Well, Myron, there really was no actual harm done here. I don't like the fact that your boy was following my daughter around with his drone, but new technology brings new behavior expectations to all of us. Can I have your word, Stanley, that you'll knock it off?"

Stanley nodded his head, but when his dad nudged him with his foot, Stanley said, "Yes, Mr. Pearl, I can assure you I will no longer follow Ginni with my drone nor shine lights in the backyard."

"And what about the petitions?" asked Stanley's dad.

"Well . . ." Dad slowly began. "If Stanley wants some credit for helping a good cause, then perhaps he should work for it. I think he should join Ginni, Frankie, and Neelia when they're canvassing the neighborhoods getting signatures."

I almost fell off my seat when Dad said this. *How does this punish Stanley?* I shouted in my head. *The only ones being punished are Frankie and me!*

"We have only four more days to knock on doors," Dad went on. "I have a meeting with Mr. Snidely on the 26th. But that's enough time for Stanley to get a feeling of what it's like trooping around in the cold on a mission."

"Jim, you've been more than fair and understanding," Stanley's dad said as he motioned for Stanley to stand up and walk toward the front door. "Tomorrow, then, right after school. And that drone will be packed away for a good long time. He *might* get it back before high school graduation," he said with a bit of a twinkle in his eye.

Stanley groaned as he and his father left the house.

"Dad, how could you?" I exclaimed as soon as they left. I was just about in tears. "You know how Stanley is mean to us all the time. You just saddled Frankie and me with four days of torture!"

Dad came over to me, wrapped his arms around me, and held me tight. After a minute, he said, "I truly think that Stanley will not be his normal self on this venture, or I wouldn't have set it up. I think he's embarrassed, and the last thing he'll want to do is to get himself into any more trouble. Myron and I talked about this on the phone before he even came over, and we decided together on the punishments. He promised me he will lay down the law with Stanley before you guys head out tomorrow. And here's your backup plan. If Stanley says one mean or teasing thing to either of you, you immediately call me on your cell phone and tell me where you are. I will come and get Stanley and deliver him to his father, which I know Stanley will not want to happen. Let's give it a shot, okay?"

It frustrated me that Dad (like Mom) could be so forgiving. But I had to admit he had thought out a good plan. I looked over at Frankie, who nodded his head. With a sigh, I told Dad we'd give it a shot.

I hugged Dad back. Since it was now too late to go out for more signatures, we simply ate a light dinner and enjoyed a movie with popcorn and Dad's best hot cocoa ever. All the while, I did my best to forget how much I dreaded going out tomorrow with Stanley.

CHAPTER 12

THE MEETING WITH MR. SNIDELY

I hate to admit it, but Dad was right again. During the four days we went out to get the last of the signatures, Stanley completely behaved himself. I was still carrying Mr. Whiskers, and I wondered if Stanley wasn't still a bit scared of him and maybe that's why he wasn't goofing around. By the fourth day, Stanley had taken over the job of reading the speech on the index card, which was great because it had gotten a little tiring saying the same thing over and over. When we said goodbye after we knocked on the last door, I was ever so relieved to be done.

It was now the day of the big meeting at Mr. Snidely's office. Dad, Georgina, Frankie, Neelia, and I were going to meet with Mr. Snidely in his office right after school. How I got through the school day, I'll never know.

As usual, I met Frankie right after the dismissal bell rang, and we almost ran home. We flung our backpacks on the floor and were about to grab Neelia and walk to Pearly White Dentistry when Dad stepped out of his home office.

"Why are you here?" I asked. "Is everything okay? Are we still meeting with Mr. Snidely?"

"Yes, Ginni, everything is fine. I took the afternoon off. I thought it best if we drive to Mr. Snidely's office rather than walk. We don't want to appear rushed. We are going to pick Georgina up at her store, then head over. Her assistant is going to keep the store open while we have our meeting. You guys ready to go?"

I was so nervous, I couldn't answer, but I nodded my head. Frankie didn't seem to be as worried about things as I was. He simply stood there snuggling Neelia, waiting for us all to head out to the car.

Before we left, I ran upstairs to give Mr. Whiskers a quick pat on his head. "This is it," I told him. "Wish us luck." He squeaked loudly while running on his wheel as I left the bedroom.

It took less than three minutes to drive to the back door of the chocolate shop. Georgina saw us coming and opened the door wide. "Come in for a moment while I get my coat," she said.

Frankie just stood there on the sidewalk holding Neelia, not daring to come in.

As soon as Georgina realized what he was doing, she gave a small laugh and bent down to hug both Frankie and Neelia. I could hear her say kindly to Frankie, "It's okay; Neelia can come in too, since we'll be going right back outside." And then she gave Neelia a kiss on her cheek and got a friendly meow in response.

We were all fairly dressed up for the occasion, and it seemed odd for the five of us, Dad carrying his brief-case, to be marching off to the cellular store. We must have been a sight, but thankfully we didn't have far to go.

During our short walk, I kept repeating to myself, *Believe, always Believe . . .*

When we walked in, one salesclerk recognized us and took us to Mr. Snidely's back office.

It was a tiny office. File cabinets, a large desk, and two visitor chairs filled the room completely. I thought, *No wonder he needs to expand!* before I shook my head to stop myself from feeling sorry for Mr. Snidely's stuffed office.

Without even a "good afternoon," Mr. Snidely began. "I know why you're both here, Jim and Georgina. I've seen all the signs around town, and I've heard the buzz. You think you can get me to change my mind about your eviction simply with a few signatures on pieces of paper? I am completely within my legal right to evict you. I'm sorry, but business is business. As you can see, things are cramped around here. I'm ready to bring a state-of-the-art cell phone store to the citizens of Makawee, and they will be thankful that I will now be able to offer them all the latest and greatest!"

Georgina said nothing but looked defeated as she sat in her chair with her head bowed. Dad sat in the other chair. Frankie, holding Neelia, stood next to Dad, and I was next to Frankie.

Dad was anything but defeated. I've never seen him act so strong and sure of himself. I was filled with pride as he began.

"Mr. Snidely, I have the signatures of 7,452 people who are of a different opinion," Dad said while laying out the impressive stack of papers. "What you may not realize is that Georgina's chocolate shop is a beloved store. In fact, if you don't know Makawee's history, a chocolate shop has existed in that location since 1919.

It is one of a handful of stores that have lasted generation after generation. My parents and my grandparents both loved that chocolate shop, and since Georgina took it over several years ago, she's done nothing but make it better with a cool website, online ordering, and new tasty treats added frequently. Tradition means a great deal to the citizens of Makawee, and I'd hate to see you lose business by making people angry that you've closed their beloved chocolate shop."

"Hogwash!" Mr. Snidely retorted. "Oh, sure, there'll be an editorial or two in the paper saying, 'Boo hoo, we've lost our candy store,' but after a short time, that'll all die down. Especially when people get wind of the latest phones, accessories, coverage plans, and all the tech toys I have on display. Pretty soon they won't even remember that there was a chocolate shop there!"

I was thinking we were doomed. People do like their tech toys—hadn't I been thrilled just two months ago when I got my own cell phone?

Georgina was making motions like she was getting ready to leave, and even Dad didn't have an immediate comeback to Mr. Snidely's sharp remarks. It was then that Neelia leapt out of Frankie's arms and walked across the desk in front of Mr. Snidely.

Unconsciously, Mr. Snidely started petting Neelia while she looked directly into his eyes. "And I'll tell you one more thing . . ." as his voice trailed off.

"People want . . .

People want . . .

People want . . .

"Chocolate! That's what people want!"

Immediately Georgina lifted her head. Dad leaned back in his chair, and Frankie just grinned.

Neelia put her paws on Mr. Snidely's face and licked his cheek while he continued to pet her head.

"What did I just say?" asked Mr. Snidely.

"You said, 'People want chocolate,' Mr. Snidely," said Dad. "But people also want their tech toys!"

Georgina, Frankie, and I stared at Dad. Was he about to blow this? What was he doing?

"I know just the thing," Dad continued. "There's a small business area being developed by Industrial Park, just south of town. How about building an additional store there before someone else does? Not only will you maintain your foothold as the main cell phone provider in Makawee, but you could have as big a store as you want. I hear they are offering special rates to businesses right now to encourage expansion. And at your new mega store, your customers will have easy parking as well. Perhaps you'll even want to expand to computers, tablets, and other tech devices."

"I like it!" Mr. Snidely exclaimed as he picked up Neelia and gave her a kiss on her cheek. He stood up, still holding Neelia, and shook hands with everyone in the room, including Frankie and me. "I'll make the contacts this afternoon."

We were getting ready to leave when Frankie gave a little cough.

"Oh, yes," laughed Mr. Snidely, "you'll want your kitten back. Extraordinary creature." Frankie was standing right there waiting for Mr. Snidely to place Neelia in his arms.

"And Georgina," Mr. Snidely said, waiting for her to turn around. When she did, he picked up the eviction notice and tore it in half. Georgina, overcome with happiness, rushed to Mr. Snidely and gave him a great big hug. I don't think Mr. Snidely had been hugged very often before. He turned fifteen shades of red and even got tears in the corner of his eyes before she let him go.

The clerks all stared at us in disbelief as we left the store. We heard Mr. Snidely shout out to them with a laugh, "Forget the chocolate shop, gang, we're building a whole new store!"

"We are going to celebrate," exclaimed Georgina once we were back in her shop. "I'm taking us all to Jerry's to celebrate with an early dinner!"

"You don't have to take us," countered Dad, "but I agree, this calls for a celebration!"

Dad and Mom had always gone to Jerry's for celebratory dinners—like on their anniversary. It was a fancy place that we only went to on special occasions, and this for sure was a special occasion!

"We'll argue about the bill later; for now, we are going to enjoy," said Georgina. "I'm just sorry we can't take Neelia. She's the one who made this happen."

"We all made this happen, Georgina. Beginning with you. If people didn't love what you've done with the store since you took over, we'd never have been able to get so many signatures. Neelia will be thanked in her own way," Dad said.

Dinner was marvelous! We had onion rings for an appetizer, and all of us had salads and steaks with au gratin potatoes. My steak was so tender, I could almost cut it with my fork. We were having ice cream sundaes for dessert when Jerry himself came over. "I heard the good news!" he exclaimed. "Congratulations! I want you to know that all of your dinners are on the house."

"We couldn't possibly," argued both Georgina and Dad.

"I insist," continued Jerry. "What happened to you was scary for all business owners. The way you banded together and stood up to Mr. Snidely is a model for every one of us. A dinner is the least I can do."

What was it that Ms. Nineon said at the school Valentine's Day assembly? I thought. Learn from your mistakes and do something that will help make the world a better place and see what happens when we all work together. And you may even get rewarded for your good deeds.

If we hadn't made a mistake by bringing Neelia into the candy store, and if Dad hadn't helped us right that wrong by organizing the petition (which brought the entire town together), then my guess is that Georgina, instead of enjoying a steak dinner on the house tonight, would instead be packing up her store. Ms. Nineon sure does know a thing or two, I thought with a smile.

Before I went to bed that night, I took some leftover yarn and quickly knit Mr. Whiskers a tiny mouse-sized scarf to match the one I'd carried him around in when we were petitioning. When I dropped his new scarf in his cage, he immediately curled it around his neck. How he knew to do that, I'll never know, but boy, did he look cute!

REOPENING CELEBRATION

CHAPTER 13

PARTY!

On Saturday, March 1—the day she was to have been evicted, and just two days after the meeting with Mr. Snidely—Georgina hosted a Reopening Celebration party at her shop. She had put a huge notice in the paper, a banner headline on her website, and signs all around town to announce the party.

When Dad, Frankie, and I got there, the place was packed. Tons of people stood around munching on meat and cheese, specialty nut mixtures, fruit salad, and of course, chocolates! Georgina had decorated the store in a grand style, and she was beaming with pride.

Lots of people I knew were there. I saw the mayor of Makawee, Dr. Little, the entire Pebbles family, Irving from Handyman's Hardware, Jerry, and even Mr. Snidely. And, believe it or not, Mr. Snidely was happily talking to a great number of people, all excited about building his new mega store south of town.

When I spotted Georgina, she was talking to Stanley and his dad. I slyly took a few steps toward them, and I was amused to overhear Stanley boasting about all the work he had done to collect signatures. Sure, he had been of some help, but he made it sound like he'd done it all by himself. I smiled as I shook my head at Stanley being Stanley.

I couldn't help but feel a bit of pride that Frankie

and I had been part of believing and making this all happen. I gave a little nod to heaven to ask Mom if she was proud of her little girl. Somehow, my heart immediately felt even more full of love. Yes, I knew Mom was proud of us all.

When Georgina saw us, she came directly over and asked that we go home and get Neelia and bring her to the back door. "Of course," Frankie and I said, a bit confused.

When we got home, I went to my bedroom where I told Mr. Whiskers that he was coming with me, but he had to stay hidden in my scarf pocket. *Mr. Whiskers deserves to celebrate, too*, I thought. He looked at me as if he understood. I was in such a good mood, I went bumpity-bump down our curved staircase. Frankie had already harnessed Neelia, so we headed out. And, of course, Tyto was following us.

In a few minutes, we were back at the chocolate shop. We knocked on the back door, and Georgina and Dad opened the door and let us in. From the back office, you could hear all the party noises. It felt odd, like we weren't supposed to be there.

Georgina took Neelia from Frankie's arms and held her up over her head. "Neelia," Georgina said, "I felt terrible that you couldn't join us at Jerry's for our celebration, so I wanted to do something nice for you. I have a present." And with that, she stepped aside and set Neelia down next to a tray with a water bowl and a food dish. I could see that something was engraved on it, but I couldn't quite make it out. When I bent down to get a better look, I saw that the food dish said "Neelia" and the water bowl said "My Savior."

"And, Frankie and Ginni," Georgina went on to say, "Neelia is welcome here anytime, but you guys have to come to the back door, and Neelia has to stay back here where she won't upset any customers. Deal?" Georgina picked up Neelia again, and Neelia answered with a meow and a lick on Georgina's cheek.

"And, Neelia," Georgina continued, "thank you for curing a grump!"

PUBLIC LIBRARY

COMING UP . . .

Be sure to follow Ginni, Frankie, Neelia, Tyto, and Mr. Whiskers on their next adventure, *The Kitten Who Scared a Ghost.*

Research Horror. That's what the fourth graders secretly call their spring research project. The town's two librarians, Mrs. Curtz and Mrs. Gynther, along with their teacher, Ms. Zinger, assign this project to the class one early March morning.

This is going to mean extra trips to the public library and computer lab, Ginni thinks. She wonders if she has the courage to do her report on Amelia Earhart. Ginni's mother, an Air Force pilot, had been shot down last summer while on a mission. Would writing a report on Ms. Earhart help Ginni heal—or would it be too painful?

But when Ginni and Frankie troop to the public library, they are surprised to learn that the library is now haunted.

Ginni and Frankie don't believe in ghosts, or so they think. But if it's not a ghost, then what is making all those weird noises? Countless people have investigated and found nothing—but then, they didn't have Neelia to help them.

ACKNOWLEDGMENTS

To family and friends who have taken their time to read both books and provide valuable feedback. And especially to Colin, my youngest reviewer – thank you for helping me see the story through young eyes. Everyone's time and efforts are greatly valued.

To my team at DartFrog – I appreciate all everyone has done to help bring Neelia and her friends to life!

ABOUT THE AUTHOR

Nova DuBois has spent her life among children's books and elementary-aged children. She began her love of children's literature in her early teens when volunteering at her hometown's library where she held Saturday morning storytelling hour and assisted in maintaining the children's book area. This passion resulted in pre- and post-graduate degrees in library science. She enjoys bringing stories to life for children and watching their imaginations soar.

She has her own special black cat who helps provide inspiration for the *Vine Street Mysteries* series. This is the second book of this series, and who knows where her black cat will lead her?

CPSIA information can be obtained
at www.ICGtesting.com
Printed in the USA
LVHW020935250222
711994LV00024B/1429

9 781956 019544